Date: 1/14/14

LP FIC COBLE
Coble, Colleen.
Holy night : an Aloha Reef
Christmas novella /

HOLY NIGHT

This Large Print Book carries the
Seal of Approval of N.A.V.H.

HOLY NIGHT

AN ALOHA REEF CHRISTMAS NOVELLA

COLLEEN COBLE

THORNDIKE PRESS
A part of Gale, Cengage Learning

GALE
CENGAGE Learning®

Detroit • New York • San Francisco • New Haven, Conn • Waterville, Maine • London

GALE
CENGAGE Learning®

© 2013 by Colleen Coble.
Thorndike Press, a part of Gale, Cengage Learning.

Thorndike Press® Large Print Christian Fiction.
The text of this Large Print edition is unabridged.
Other aspects of the book may vary from the original edition.
Set in 16 pt. Plantin.

LIBRARY OF CONGRESS CATALOGING-IN-PUBLICATION DATA

Coble, Colleen.
    Holy night : an Aloha Reef Christmas novella / by Colleen Coble. -- Large print edition.
    pages ; cm. -- (Thorndike Press large print Christian fiction)
    ISBN 978-1-4104-6329-6 (hardcover) -- ISBN 1-4104-6329-X (hardcover) 1. Hawaii--Fiction. 2. Christmas stories. 3. Large type books. I. Title.
PS3553.O2285H65 2013b
813'.54--dc23   2013040125

Published in 2013 by arrangement with Thomas Nelson, Inc.

Printed in the United States of America
1 2 3 4 5 6 7 18 17 16 15 14

HOLY NIGHT

ONE

The fresh aroma of the sea was welcome after the stale air of the airplane. Leia Kahale inhaled, then swept her arm toward the broad expanse of the golden sand of Shipwreck Beach on Kaua'i's south shore. The waves were always treacherous here, but strong swells had been battering the island for three days and few people were in the water.

She pointed. "We could put the tent up here, Bane. I'd love for

Makawehi Point to loom in the back for great wedding pictures. And with poinsettias, it will be just perfect."

Her fiancé, Bane Oana, draped his muscular arm around her shoulders. He wore black board shorts and a turquoise aloha shirt that looked good with his black hair. "Whatever you want, honey."

Leia lifted her face into the warm December breeze. Her heart felt full to bursting as she pressed against Bane's warm chest. "It seems almost wrong to be this happy."

Bane smiled down at her. "I haven't had any trouble adjusting to our new normal." He brushed a kiss across her lips. "I like your curves in that dress. I might have to fight off the other men on the beach."

The way her skin heated at his touch never failed to thrill her. How could one person affect her so dramatically? She held his face and kissed him again. "Do you know how much I've missed you?"

Bane's younger sister, Kaia, nudged him, breaking their kiss. She tucked her long dark hair behind her ears. "Hey, you two, we have work to do. Less kissing, more planning. The wedding is in five days. There are a ton of details to see to. Bane, I need you to run by The Beach House and pay for the rehearsal reception, then stop and pay the catering bill. Leia and I will show the staff where we want the tent and tables."

He groaned. "My fiancée just arrived from Moloka'i and I have to leave her to write checks?" He didn't drop his arm from around Leia.

"That would be a good guess." Kaia smiled and patted his arm.

Leia smiled and tipped her face up for another kiss. His spicy scent made her heart speed up. Heat rushed to her cheeks at the realization they would only be apart a few more nights. "Talk to you tonight. Wait, when does Mano arrive?"

"About five. I'll pick him up, and we'll meet you at Kaia's for dinner." He lifted Leia in his arms. "Or maybe I'll just take you with me."

She laughed and kissed him again. "Put me down, you big oaf. We have work to do."

He sighed. "You know what they say about all work and no play. Look at that surf. It's just begging for a board."

"And we'll go surfing. But later." She smiled as he put her feet back on the ground. "And I'll fix you lomilomi salmon tonight to make it up to you."

His expression brightened. "I'll wax the board when I'm done. Don't be too late." He walked across the thick sand toward the Jeep parked in the lot across the street.

"Leia, look at this!" Her sister,

Eva, waved to her from a tide pool. "There's a starfish." Her beautiful blond hair turned men's heads wherever she went until they noticed her Down syndrome features.

"In a minute, Eva." Leia ignored Eva's pout and turned back to face Kaia. "I love Bane so much, but I'm a little nervous. Will I be a good wife and mother? I mean, I didn't really have a great role model."

Kaia smiled and squeezed Leia's hand. "You know about giving to other people. You've practically raised Eva yourself, and look what a good job you've done with her. You and my brother are great together."

Leia sighed. "You're right. I know

we are. It's just —"

A scream pierced the air behind them and a board shot up in the roiling waves off the beach. Then a hand waved.

Leia pointed out a dark head. "Someone's in trouble."

"Go get the lifeguard from the Hyatt!" someone yelled.

Kaia kicked off her OluKai slippers and ran for the heavy surf. Everyone on the beach gathered to watch as she plunged into the big waves and struck out toward the figure. She worked with dolphins and was an excellent swimmer, almost more at home in the water than on the land.

Leia joined the crowd and held her breath, praying all the while.

Kaia reached the area where the hand had gone up, but the woman couldn't be seen. Kaia dove into the water, and seconds went by in an agonizing trickle until two heads popped up in the surf.

Only then did Leia exhale. She kicked off her slippers, then rushed to help Kaia bring the woman ashore. It would be a tricky exit from the sea here with the tide adding to the ocean's power. Kaia got close enough to stand, and she steadied the woman she'd just rescued, clearly a tourist from the beet-red sunburn on her face and arms.

Leia waded out a few feet, though it was all she could do to stand when the waves slammed into her.

She licked her salty lips and watched for a break in the surf.

Kaia spoke to the woman, who nodded. Then, looking at the sea, Kaia grabbed her arm and propelled her toward the shore at the right time. As they neared, Leia took the woman's other arm and helped her as they staggered to the sand. The woman collapsed, and Kaia stood panting as a lifeguard rushed up.

The woman sobbed hysterically as the lifeguard checked her over. "I almost drowned." She looked up at Kaia. "Thank you, thank you."

"Glad I was able to help. You'll be all right."

Leia retreated a few more steps as a paramedic arrived. She glanced around for Eva. The tide pool where she'd been splashing was deserted. Leia moved toward the crowd. Eva might have been watching the rescue. But after two minutes Leia still hadn't caught sight of her sister's blond head.

Maybe she'd gone to get something to drink. Leia hurried to the Hyatt, but there was no one around the outdoor lagoon or the drink area. She retraced her steps to find Kaia standing by their abandoned shoes with a towel someone had given her. "Kaia, I can't find Eva."

Her friend frowned. "She has to be here somewhere."

"Maybe the excitement frightened her. She could be back at your car."

"Let's go check."

The women hurried past the Hyatt's main entrance to the parking lot. The little red Volkswagen Kaia drove was empty. Leia stopped a couple putting their things away in a van. "Have you seen a blond woman about twenty-three? She has Down syndrome and she was wearing a red sundress."

The woman, about forty with pudgy legs sticking out of her shorts, nodded. "I did just see her. She was with a man."

Leia's gut clenched. "Where did they go?" Eva trusted everyone, and Leia had to watch carefully to make sure men didn't take advantage of her.

The woman pointed. "Up the

cliff."

Makawehi Cliff was a popular place with the locals to jump into the water, though it was dangerous, especially on a day like today. Eva would never do that on her own, even on a calm day.

Kaia started that way. "I'll check there, *mahalo*. Leia, you stay here in case she's just in the restroom or something. She'll panic if she can't find you." Kaia started across the parking lot toward the cliff.

"Hope you find her." The woman got in the van with her husband.

Dread congealed in Leia's stomach as she looked around the lot. A scrap of paper on the wipers caught her eye, and she stepped to the Volkswagen and retrieved it. She unfolded the note. The words jumped out at her and nearly drove her to her knees.

I have Eva. If you call the police, you'll find her dead body. If you tell Kaia or Bane, you'll find her body. Wait.

The paid catering bill was tucked in the pocket of Bane's board shorts when he walked into Tomkats. He smiled as his favorite cat sidled up and wound around his legs. The scent of macadamia-encrusted mahimahi filled the space. A few locals and several tourists glanced up when he walked in, then went back to their meals. The tables were decorated for Christmas, and potted poinsettias added color to the plants growing in the courtyard.

He glanced around for his younger brother. He'd dropped Mano here while he stopped by the caterer's. Mano beckoned to him from a table in the back by the window. Broad and capable, Mano looked every inch a former Navy SEAL. He lifted his soft drink in Bane's direction. "You seem calm for a man about to be married. I thought Annie would have a nervous breakdown before our wedding. The craziness hasn't hit yet?"

Bane pulled out a chair and sat. "Leia is pretty calm about it all. We both are." He eyed his brother. "You've got that flat mouth. What's going on?"

Whenever Mano was dealing with something unpleasant, he pressed his lips together and didn't look Bane in the face. Mano ducked his head.

"Mano? Everything okay with Annie?"

His brother's head came up then. "Oh sure, Annie is great." He heaved a sigh. "I guess you have to know. They released Zimmer."

Bane straightened. "When?"

"Last week."

"And they're just now telling us?" Bane flopped back in his chair. "Don't they realize he's dangerous? Why didn't I get a call?"

"The DA called the house when they couldn't get you on your cell. You were probably diving. I took the call."

Bane was an oceanographer and did sea salvage. He was often where his cell phone didn't work. Dennis Zimmer, a name he'd tried not to think about the past few years. He and Zimmer had been friends once, but Bane had caught the ex–Coast Guard ensign stealing supplies and selling them. A Coast Guard seaman had been killed in the last heist. Bane had found the evidence and had been forced to testify against Zimmer, who was convicted of robbery and manslaughter.

He exhaled. "Is he headed this way?"

"The DA suspected he might be. When did you get the last letter from him?"

Bane thought back. "About a year ago, I think. I need to warn Leia to be careful." He rose. "I'd better go talk to the police and see if they can keep an eye on flights into Kaua'i."

"You haven't even eaten."

"I'm suddenly not very hungry." Bane strode out the door toward where he'd parked his Jeep.

He yanked open the door and slid inside. When he slammed the door, he realized the truck was tilted to the left like it was on something. He got back out and glanced at the tires on the right. They looked fine so he went around to the other side. Two tires rested on their rims. Closer inspection showed they'd been slashed.

The blood rushed from his head. Zimmer was already here.

TWO

Wait. But Leia couldn't just wait here for some unknown person to call her, not when she felt like she'd just downed fifteen cups of coffee. And what was taking Kaia so long to climb the cliff and get back?

Leia stared at the note. How could this kidnapper even ask her to keep it from the man she loved? She couldn't handle this without Bane.

Maybe it was someone trying to scare her. She eyed the Hyatt. Eva could be in there chatting away with someone. Or she could have spotted a monk seal down the beach and gone to see it. She prayed this was a hoax of some kind, someone's idea of a weird joke.

Slinging her bright orange beach bag over her shoulder, she started back to the beach. Her cell phone chirped in her bag, and she dropped to her knees and dug for it. Her heart pounded as it rang four times, then five, before her fingers closed around it.

"Hello?" Her voice was breathless. "Eva?"

"Eva is fine. For now." The distorted voice on the other end had to be from a machine. "But if you don't do exactly as I say, you'll find her body under the Point. Dead."

"Don't hurt her." Leia licked her dry lips. "She's like a child."

"Then you'll do what I say. Go find lover boy and tell him you've got cold feet. You don't want to marry him after all."

Leia gripped the phone with a damp hand. "What? Why?"

"When you've done what I say and the wedding date is past, I'll release your sister."

"B-But that's five days away!" Leia's voice shook. "She'll be terrified. You have to let her go. Please, I'll do anything!"

"Then do what I tell you. And no police. Tell no one you've received this call. If you simply change the wedding date, I'll know. Make Bane believe you or Eva will be dead."

"You're asking me to do the impossible," she whispered. "Everyone will want to know where Eva is. Kaia is looking for her right now."

"When Kaia gets back, tell her you got a call from Eva asking if she could stay with a friend for a few days."

"No one will believe that!"

There was a pause. "Then come up with a story they *will* believe. Your sister's life is resting on you."

"Please, just let Eva go." Her eyes burning with the effort to hold back her tears, Leia paced the lot.

The call ended and she stared at her phone. This could not be happening. She scrolled through the received calls, but the last call was from a blocked number. No way to call him back.

Her knees went weak and she sank to the pavement. The hot concrete burned into her flesh, but even that pain didn't come close to the agony squeezing her lungs. The man had put her in an impossible position. She saw no way of convincing anyone that Eva was fine. And Bane would never believe she didn't want to marry him.

Yes, he will.

She'd dragged her feet long enough, making excuses for putting off the wedding. First it had been she couldn't desert her grandmother as she was making plans to move into an assisted-living place. Then she had to sell her *kapa* business, and that had taken awhile. The base of all of it was fear, plain and simple. She'd buried herself in her little town on Moloka'i, happy to be in her element with people she knew. But as Bane's wife, they'd be traveling, meeting new people. Bane had been patient with her, but if she told him she'd changed her mind, he would think she didn't love him. Their past would be enough to convince him. She'd sent him away once before.

Her thoughts scattered like pikake petals in a hurricane. She had to convince the man she loved that she didn't want to marry him. How could she hurt him like that? But she had to do it to save Eva.

Kaia waved at her from the base of the cliff. Her face was pink from exertion, and her dark eyes were strained as she came toward Leia. "Eva jumped off the cliff with a man, but I can't find her."

Leia gasped, and spots danced in front of her eyes. How was that possible? She'd just talked to him. Could there be more than one person involved? "D-Did anyone see her after that?"

Kaia shook her head. "Let's look along the beach. Most people jump off that thing with no trouble."

Leia swallowed hard and squared her shoulders. "She knows better than to do that."

Kaia nodded and put her hand on

Leia's arm. "If we can't find her, we have to call the Coast Guard. You know that."

"I-I know. But she'll be all right. I know she's all right."

"Of course she is." But Kaia's glance slid away. "Let's go look."

Tears finally escaped Leia's eyes. "Pray, Kaia."

Kaia took her hand. "I haven't stopped."

The sun was setting over the ocean to the west, bouncing rays of gold and pink off the water. Bane's stomach burned sourly. They'd walked two miles, all the way to Maha'ulepu Beach, a remote stretch of sand frequented only by locals. Still no sign of Eva. A Coast

Guard cutter cruised offshore as well. Kaia and her husband, Jesse, were on another boat with Kaia's bottle-nosed dolphin, Nani. If Eva was out there, Nani would find her.

Eva could have been washed out to sea.

Or drowned.

He stepped closer to Leia, who stood on a rock at the edge of the water. She barely took her attention off the whitecaps rolling toward the golden sand. "We'll find her, honey." He put more confidence into his voice than he felt.

Tears shimmered in her eyes when she glanced at him before turning her attention back to the water. "I should have been watching her, Bane."

"There was a near drowning, Leia. Of course you and Kaia wanted to help." A wave soaked his feet as he waded in closer to her and slipped his arm around her waist. "We're not doing her any good here. Let's go back to Shipwreck Beach and head the other direction."

"Mano and Annie went that way. They'll call if they find her." She glanced at him again. "Any word from Kaia?"

"She called a few minutes ago. Nani hasn't found anything."

She sagged against him, then turned and buried her face in his chest. He held her close without saying a word. What was there to say? They'd lived in the islands all their lives. No one knew the dangers of the sea better than the two of them. The muscles in her back were rigid and unyielding as if she was holding herself apart from him.

He stroked his hand along her spine and wished he could comfort her somehow. He still needed to tell her about Zimmer too. For all he knew, the man could be despicable enough to seek revenge by hurting Leia.

She pulled away and wiped her eyes. The sun sank faster now, plunging into the water like a fireball. "We'll ride back with Kaia and Jesse on the boat. It will be too dark to see the potholes in the lane. Look, they're coming in now for us."

She nodded and let him lead her into the water as the roar of Jesse's boat grew nearer. Nani swam up to them, chirping her friendly hello, and Bane rubbed her warm, rubbery body before helping Leia climb the ladder to the boat. He clambered aboard himself and moved to drop into a seat by his sister.

How's Leia? Kaia mouthed.

He winced and shook his head. His gaze found Leia where she sat with her head down. When she was like that, it was tough to get through the remoteness she'd pulled around her. She barely looked up when he moved to sit by her.

He took her hand, so cold and

motionless. "Honey, talk to me. We have to hold to each other through this."

Her eyes were wide and unblinking. "This is my fault."

"You're just upset."

"No, I need to do a better job with Eva. If I hadn't been distracted . . . I don't think I can marry you, Bane. Eva needs me too much."

"Of course you can marry me. We'll find Eva and things will be back to normal soon. You'll see. Eva loves me. She wouldn't want to go back to life without me there. You know that as well as I do."

"I don't know." Leia exhaled with a rush of air, then turned her head and looked out over the dark sea.

The tight line of her pressed lips broke his heart.

"Maybe she came ashore somewhere. She might be wandering around lost. Her picture will be on the news tonight and in the paper. Someone will see her."

She shook her head. "I realize now this marriage is not the right thing for any of us." She pulled her hand away, then wrenched off her ring and handed it to him. "I'm not going to marry you, Bane. I'm sorry." The last word ended on a sob.

His fingers closed around the ring she pressed into his hand. He stared into her face. What was she thinking? This wasn't happening. She loved him. But staring into her remote eyes, he saw no spark of the constant love he was used to seeing.

He put the ring in his pocket. "We'll talk about it after we find Eva. You're just upset, and I don't blame you."

"I blame me," she whispered. "I should have known better."

Was she punishing herself — and him — for Eva's disappearance? He slipped his arm around her and tipped her face up to his. His lips found hers and his pulse sped at the way she kissed him back.

Then she jerked away. "Just because we have passion between us doesn't mean we belong together."

If that was how she felt, he didn't know her anymore. He gave her a

long look, then moved to his side
of the bench.

THREE

The clock on the bed stand showed 12:02, but a rooster still crowed in the dark beyond her window. A breeze blew in the scent of ginger from the flower bed outside. Leia lay on the guest bed at Kaia's with her eyes wide open. How could she sleep with Eva in such danger? And she kept replaying the hurt in Bane's eyes. She moaned and threw her hand over her eyes.

Her life had seemed so perfect. How could everything fall apart so quickly? She had to find Eva and get her back safely.

She sat up and swung her legs to the floor. Maybe some chamomile tea would help her sleep. She padded across the wood floor to the door. She put her hand on the doorknob, but her cell phone rang, a blaring sound in the still of the night. She leaped for the nightstand and snatched it up, sparing a glance at the display.

Blocked.

Her throat tightened. It was him. "Hello?"

"You haven't called off the wedding."

The electronically altered voice gave her chills. She tightened her grip on the phone. "I did! I gave him back his ring."

"The food has not been canceled."

She sank onto the edge of the bed. "They were closed by the time we finished searching for Eva."

He said nothing for a long minute. "If the food isn't canceled by noon, look for Eva's body."

A mental image came of Eva's long blond hair floating around her lifeless body. Leia choked back a wave of nausea. "I'll do it when they open at nine. Please. Don't hurt her."

"I don't like it when someone plays games with me."

She bit her lip. "I'm not playing games. I told you — there was a search going on for Eva, and I couldn't do anything about the food. They believed she might have drowned, and it was easier to let them think that rather than she'd gone off with a friend."

"I'll give you one more chance. Don't screw this up."

When the call dropped, she lowered her hand and stared at her phone. Could there be a way to trace him? She tossed her phone onto the bed. He'd said not to tell the police, but she was so ill equipped to find Eva by herself. Could she even trust him to follow through on his promise to release her sister? What if she did everything exactly as he said, but he killed Eva anyway? Leia would never be able to live with the regret.

She moaned and put her head in her hands. What should she do? No matter what she decided, it could all go horribly wrong.

She lifted her head at a soft knock on the door. "Yes?"

"It's me." Bane's deep voice spoke on the other side of the door.

She grabbed her robe and pulled it on over her shorty pj's before opening the door. "What's wrong?"

"I wanted to talk and I heard you on the phone. Who was calling so late?"

She stiffened until she realized that of course he had the right to ask that kind of question. What could she say? She looked into his warm brown eyes, alight with love and concern for her. How could she put him through what that evil man demanded? Couldn't they work through this together? Wasn't that what married couples did?

He took a step closer, and his warm palm enveloped her cheek. She closed her eyes and relished the heat that spread down her neck to her belly. She loved him so much. How could she go on with this lie? Because that's what it was. Withholding the full truth was just as much a lie.

He rubbed his thumb over her skin. "I know you love me, Leia. Even now I can feel it. I have your ring in my pocket. Let's put it back on your finger."

She opened her eyes and studied him. Everything in her warred over what to do. "I can't do that, Bane. I wish I could. Th-There's . . ."

He dropped his hand and turned away before she could get out the words she needed to say. He moved toward the door, but she grabbed his arm and spun him around. When he turned to face her, she threw her arms around his neck and pressed her lips against his. She needed to feel his passion, needed his strength and wisdom.

He stood still for a moment, then his arms went around her waist, and he pulled her close. The stubble on his face rasped against the tender skin of her face, but she didn't care.

Heat flared over her skin, and he wrapped his hand through the loose hair trailing down to her waist. Her hands clutched his shirt and she closed her eyes and willed herself to forget the dire circumstances, just for a minute. All that mattered in the moment was his warm breath mingling with hers and the firm assurance of his embrace.

She made a small sound of protest when his lips left hers, then opened her eyes. His expression was hard to read in the dimly lit room.

He retreated a few feet. "What's going on, Leia? One minute you push me away and the next you're kissing me l-like that."

She inhaled, knowing in that moment she couldn't live without him. "Eva's been kidnapped."

Bane shook his head to clear it. "What are you talking about?"

He couldn't take his eyes off her with her brown hair spilling over her shoulders. He'd loved her for so long, but since this afternoon, he wasn't sure he knew her as well as he thought he did. His lips still tingled from her kiss. He stared into her blue eyes, so filled with pain.

Kidnapped.

She wet her lips. "That was the kidnapper."

There was more she wasn't telling him. She should have run to his room the minute the guy called. Instead, he'd had to find her and she was still in her room. Almost like she'd hidden it from him.

She stepped toward him. "That's the real reason I broke our engagement. The kidnapper told me if I didn't, h-he'd kill Eva." She bit her trembling lip.

He put his hand on his head and took a step toward her. "Wait, let me get this straight. You took a call earlier today and instead of telling me about it, you broke our engagement?"

Her eyes on him, she nodded. "He threatened to kill Eva if I told you."

Raking a hand through his hair, he paced toward the window. "And you believed him? You didn't trust me enough to tell me the truth? Instead, you flippantly break my heart and push me away."

He'd been in the Coast Guard, for Pete's sake. Danger was nothing new to him. Who would be better equipped to find Eva than him? Leia must not trust him at all.

She held her hand out toward him. "It's not that at all! This is my sister's life we're talking about. He was very specific about what I had to do if I wanted to see her again."

She was so beautiful standing there in her white robe with her feet bare and her hair loose. Another week and she would be his bride. Naturally she'd been upset when this guy called.

She should have told me.

He took her hand. "Tell me exactly what he said."

She tucked a long lock behind her

ear. "His voice was electronically garbled. He said I was not to call the police, and that if I told you, we'd find Eva's body in the sea." Her voice wobbled. "Then he said I had to break the engagement if I ever wanted to see Eva again."

"This guy has something personal against me. I bet it's Zimmer."

"Who's Zimmer?"

"A scumbag I sent to jail for robbery and manslaughter. He swore he'd get revenge." He watched her flinch. "My tires were slashed this afternoon. Two of them."

"You're sure it was him?"

"Who else?" He stared at her and wished all his doubts could be erased with a kiss. "Before today, I would have sworn you believed in me, trusted me with your life."

"I do!"

He made himself take her out-stretched hand. She was dealing with enough upset today. "You should have come to me immediately. We looked for her all afternoon until dark. Yet you didn't say a word. It was all a lie. You knew she wasn't out there, yet you let me and the Coast Guard waste our time when we could have been looking for the kidnapper."

Her eyes welled and tears slipped down her face. "You're right. I was just so scared, Bane. I couldn't bear it if my actions hurt Eva. He sounded so — so deadly, and I was sure he would kill her on the spot if I didn't agree to his demands."

Her tears melted his anger, and he pulled her against his chest. "I wouldn't have shut you out like this."

"You don't understand! This is Eva. She's like a child. You know she's scared. I just want her back." She began to sob. "I know I should have told you, but I panicked. And I'm telling you now. I could have still kept it from you, but I didn't."

He smoothed her hair, fragrant with the scent of ginger, and pressed his lips against her temple. "I'm worried about Eva too. What did he say just now when he called?"

"He said he knew we didn't cancel the food order. If it's not canceled by noon, he'll kill her."

Bane stilled as he thought through what that meant. "So he's checking up on you."

She nodded. "I told him I'd cancel it at nine when they opened."

"So why tell me now?"

"I realized I was wrong," she whispered. "I can't handle this by myself. We have to find her. I can't trust that he'll keep his word."

He nodded. "We can't trust anything Zimmer says. We have to find her." Bane wheeled toward the door. "We'd better call the police."

"But what if he finds out? He'll kill her!"

He turned slowly back to face her as he thought about it. The guy did seem to be anticipating their every move, and he knew they hadn't canceled the food order. "Let me talk to Mano and Kaia about it."

He walked out the door and into the hallway. He'd have to wake up Kaia and Jesse.

FOUR

Eva sat with her feet dangling into the water. The tile decking was warm under her, and she felt a little sleepy. "Leia would like this pool." She smiled up at her new friend Chris.

Chris smiled back. "I'll invite her over."

Eva straightened and smiled. "When? I want to see her. I'm not used to her being gone. When did she say she'd be back?"

"In a few days."

Eva pooched out her lip. "She usually takes me with her."

Chris sat beside her. "I know, but you can't expect to go with her on her honeymoon. That wouldn't be fair."

Fair. Eva hadn't considered fair. "I was supposed to be in the wedding. It wasn't fair they did it without me."

"Bane was going to have to go to a new job."

Eva had heard all of that already, and it didn't make it any better that she'd been excluded. She swished her feet in the warm water and watched the swirling eddies around her toes. "There's no Christmas tree here. There should be a tree and decorations. It's the holiest holiday of all."

"I don't like Christmas." His voice was gruff.

"You have to like Christmas. Jesus was born. I love Jesus."

"Quit talking about it! There's no Christmas here."

"I don't want to talk to you anymore. You're being mean to me when I just want to see my sister." She folded her arms across her chest. Just because Chris had bought her a new bathing suit and some shorts didn't mean anything when her heart ached to see Leia.

Chris stood. "Suit yourself."

Eva didn't look up when the door to the house banged. There was a fence all the way 'round the yard, but maybe she could still get out.

If she couldn't see Leia, she could stay with Kaia. She liked Kaia and Nani, the coolest dolphin ever. She was almost human and liked swimming with her. Eva pulled her legs out of the water and stood. Glancing toward the door, she saw Chris wasn't around. She picked up her towel and wrapped it around her waist.

She trailed her fingers along the fence, hoping to find a gate. Didn't all fences have a gate somewhere? But the solid fence was six feet high and without an opening. To get out, she'd have to go through the house. Maybe Chris would be in the bathroom or bedroom. Eva went to the back door and opened it as noiselessly as she could.

Chris's voice echoed over the tiled floors. "I think we should kill her. She's driving me crazy."

Terror gripped Eva's throat. She tiptoed over the marble floors toward the front door. Ice clinked in a glass in the kitchen on the other side of the fireplace wall. Hopefully, Chris thought she was still outside. She unlocked the door and opened it, freezing when it made a squeak. The sound of soda pouring into a glass reassured her, and she eased open the door, then stepped out onto the wide plantation-style porch.

"Eva?" Chris's voice was still distant.

Not bothering to shut the door behind her, Eva bolted for the walk that went to the front gate. She wrestled with the lock, then realized she had to have a key to get out.

"Eva?" Chris was right behind her.

She whirled with her back to the gate. "I-I heard you! You said you wanted to kill me. I don't want to be dead. I don't like you anymore. You need to let me go before Bane comes. He'll be mad at you."

She lashed out a hand as Chris reached for her.

Leia, surrounded by Bane's family, sat at a secluded table on the patio at Joe's on the Green. Christmas music on steel guitars played over the loudspeakers. "My Hawaiian

Christmas" was just ending. She picked listlessly at her eggs and Spam.

Bane's shoulder brushed hers as he reached for his coffee. "I canceled the food."

"I called the florist," Kaia said. "What else?"

"The tents?" her husband, Jesse, suggested. He was a Navy officer and spoke in a clipped, no-nonsense voice. His blond hair gleamed in the sunshine.

"I took care of that," Annie said. Her quiet competence, inherited from her Japanese mother, usually calmed those around her.

It did Leia's heart good to see the way they all rallied around her. Kaia hadn't scolded her for keeping the phone call from her, though Leia had glimpsed hurt in her eyes when she heard the news. Didn't they understand this was her sister's life at risk? Surely they would have done the same thing.

She realized they were all staring at her. "Sorry, did I miss something?"

Bane slipped his arm around her. "I know it's rough on you, honey. Kaia just mentioned the guy called you shortly after he and Eva had evidently jumped off the cliff. That seems to indicate more than one person is involved."

She nodded, relaxing into his embrace. At least he wasn't acting as upset with her. "I wondered about that too."

Mano shook his head. "Not necessarily. I've jumped that cliff plenty of times, and I'm back to shore in five minutes. If he left his cell phone on the beach and called as soon as he got back, the timing would work."

"But why did Eva go with him? No one heard her scream," Annie said.

Bane's fingers tightened around Leia's arm. "You haven't been around Eva much. She trusts everyone. If he gave her a present, even a candy bar, and was nice to her, she'd think they were best buddies."

Annie winced and stared at Leia with sympathy in her eyes. "I bet it's hard to watch out for her in today's world."

"It wasn't quite so hard on Moloka'i. We know everyone, and there aren't many visitors to our area. It's very different here with so many tourists."

"We'll find her," Jesse said, his blue eyes intense. "I've informed the Navy base to be on the lookout for her, and I've instructed our patrols to keep an eye out when on the water."

"D-Did you call the police? The kidnapper specifically said no police."

She glanced around the full patio. Could he be here even now watching her? She edged away from Bane. When he lifted a brow, she shrugged. "He might be watching.

We're not supposed to be engaged any longer."

His lips flattened, but he pulled his arm back and moved away a few inches. "I didn't call them yet. We have resources to tap ourselves first, just in case he has a mole in the police department."

Mano leaned forward on his muscular forearms. "I'm going to go to the local hotels and ask around."

"And I know some real-estate people who rent to tourists. I'm going to get a list of single male renters and scope out the units."

Leia frowned. "What if there's more than one person involved?"

"You mean like a couple?" Kaia's eyes widened. "You're right. I should probably stake out every condo complex and ask for a list of rental houses."

"It's like looking for a mongoose in the weeds," Annie put in. "There are so many rental units on the island."

"I bet he's close by, though," Bane said. "He's keeping an eye on Leia. So we should only have to check out the South Shore rentals."

"I'll start with the ones on Hoona and Lawai Roads. Lots of tourists out that way, and it's quiet. A perfect place for someone to hide out," Mano said. "Some of the big homes out by Kukui'ula Harbor are rentals, and they are very private."

"And expensive," Kaia added.

Her brother shrugged. "Whoever

put this plan together has some money. It wasn't cheap to pull this off. The ticket alone would have been a thousand dollars. Add lodging, food, and rental car, and you're up to a good three grand or more."

"What about up along Omao Road? Some of those places are very private with long lanes back into the trees," Bane said.

"I'll add that to the list." Mano rose. "Annie, you come with me. We'll get a list and see what we can find out."

Annie stood but paused long enough to touch Leia's shoulder. "Try not to worry, honey. We'll get to the bottom of this."

Leia nodded. "*Mahalo* for giving me hope."

"You're one of us." Kaia rose as well. "We Oanas stick together."

The rest of the family murmured agreement as they headed out to scour the island. Leia took the last sip of her coffee. "What are we going to do?"

Bane shrugged. "It will have to be separate, though I don't like it. I don't trust this guy. He seems to be watching, though, and if we go anywhere together, he's bound to think you aren't following the rules. I'm going to follow my hunch and have the police try to find Zimmer."

He held up his hand when she opened her mouth to object. "This will not appear to have anything to do with Eva. The guy slashed my tires. When someone flies in from the mainland, they have to put on their agricultural form where they're staying and for how long. I'm hoping to track that down. It will give us some place to start."

"I didn't realize there was a form like that, but then I've never been to the mainland." She allowed a tiny spark of hope to hover in her chest. "That would be wonderful if the form said where he was staying and we had Eva back by evening!"

"I'll do all I can." Bane started to lean forward to kiss her, then checked himself. "You could walk through the area around Shipwreck in case he has her in one of the condos or rentals around Poipu Kai. She might call out to you."

"Even though she's willing to be friends with anyone, she'll be asking for me." Her eyes filled with tears. "We have to find her before another night goes by."

FIVE

Eva rubbed her arm where Chris had grabbed her. Though she kicked and screamed, he dragged her back into the house, then locked her in her room. The window was nailed shut from the outside. The bedroom wasn't for a kid like her. It was dark and dingy with a faded flowered spread. The floor was tile but it didn't look like it had been washed in a while. Leia would have gotten her mop out the minute she saw it.

Eva rubbed her wet eyes and rocked back and forth with her arms clasped around herself. She wanted her sister.

The door opened and Chris poked his head inside. She tensed before she realized he was smiling. She returned his smile tentatively. At least if he was smiling, he wasn't going to hurt her again.

"Hungry?"

Her stomach growled at the word, and she nodded. "Can I come out?"

"You promise not to try to run away again?"

She rubbed her arm. "You hurt me." She didn't like him anymore. Not even when he smiled.

His smile faded. "It was your own fault, Eva. I told you the rules. You didn't obey them, now did you?"

She hung her head. "No." Rules were important. But what if the rules were mean like his? What would Leia tell her to do?

"If you're going to be good, you can come out and eat now. I bought you some cereal."

She rose from the bed and went toward the door. "Leia fixes me eggs with runny yolks. I don't like cereal."

"Well, that's all we've got. Don't be so demanding." He gave her a shove out the door.

She scurried ahead of him to the small kitchen. At least the cereal had chocolate in it. Maybe it wouldn't be too bad. While she got down a bowl from the cabinet and pulled the milk from the fridge, he walked over and looked out the window. There weren't any other houses around. She didn't know Kaua'i very well, so she didn't know where they were. Bane had said the west side was warmer and had fewer people. Maybe that's where they were. But no, the flowers and plants in the yard were nice and green, and she hadn't seen any cactus.

Even if she'd gotten away, she wouldn't have known where to run. She forced herself to take a spoonful of cereal, but it sat like sand in her mouth. He'd be mad if she spit it out, so she managed to chew and swallow while she watched him. What if he hurt her again? She didn't like him anymore.

He saw her staring. "What? You look like you'd like to stick me with that spoon."

She folded her arms over her chest. "You're not my friend anymore."

He grinned. "Honey, I was never your friend. You're the means to an end."

She didn't know what that meant, but she didn't like his sneer. "I used to like you."

"Yeah, well, I never liked you. I'm going to make your sister and her boyfriend pay for what they did to me." He went past her to the living room.

The sunlight reflected off something metallic on the counter. His cell phone! She glanced into the living room. His back was to the doorway as he aimed the remote at the TV. She slipped from her chair and grabbed the phone, then stuck it in her bra. Returning to the table, she gulped down the rest of the tasteless cereal, then went to the doorway.

"I'm done eating now. I'm going to go to my room."

"Fine." He didn't turn around as he changed channels.

Her bare feet fairly flew down the hall, and she shut the door behind her. She tried to lock it, but he'd broken the lock on the inside. She went to the far corner and punched in her sister's number. Her pulse throbbed in her neck as it rang.

"Hello?"

The sound of Leia's voice brought tears surging to Eva's eyes. "Leia? It's me. You have to come get me. He's being mean now. I'm sorry I went with him." Her voice broke. "You told me to be careful, but he seemed so nice at first."

"Eva! Where are you, honey? I'll come get you."

"I don't know. In a house. There aren't other houses around. You have to come get me. I want to go home." She started to cry, hiccuping sounds that would bring him in to yell at her. Swallowing back the sobs, she peered out the window. He'd be so mad if he knew she'd called her sister.

"Whose phone is this?" Leia

sounded in charge and confident.

"It's his. I found it on the counter. He'll be missing it soon so I have to take it back. He'll hurt me again if he sees me with it. Come get me, Leia."

"I will, honey. We're looking for you. Don't go. What do you see out the window?"

Eva heard a noise in the hall. The doorknob began to turn. "He's coming!" She clicked off the phone and turned to face him.

The Java Kai coffee shop in Kapaa was hopping as usual, and the streets were filled with Christmas shoppers. Bane ordered a large black coffee and a Maui Mocha, then grabbed a newly vacated table outside. He'd just sat down when he spied his friend heading up the walk. "Ron, over here. I've got your mocha already."

Ron Parker was a tall whip of a man with a shock of amazingly red hair and strong features. He was out of uniform today in jeans and a black T-shirt with a Dodgers base-ball cap on backward. His smile was genuine when he spotted Bane.

Bane slid the coffee drink across the table to where Ron was seated. "You remembered, brah."

"Hard to forget a coffee drink that has coconut in it."

Ron's grin faded. "I heard about your soon-to-be sister-in-law's drowning. I'm sorry."

Bane badly wanted to tell his

friend the truth, but he bit back the confession. "*Mahalo.* We're still holding out hope she turns up. She's a really good swimmer."

"That's encouraging." Ron took a cautious sip of the hot mocha. "You said you needed my help?"

Bane nodded and leaned forward in his chair. "Did you see the report about my tires getting slashed yesterday?"

Ron shook his head. "I've been off the last couple of days. We don't see much vandalism on the island. Where did it happen?"

"In front of Tomkats."

"Wow, that's bold. Broad daylight?"

Bane nodded. "Town was a little deserted, though."

"Sundays can be that way this time of year. The biggest influx of tourists will start in another day or two." He took another sip of his mocha. "You ask around to see if anyone saw the perp?"

Bane nodded. "Called police headquarters too, and an officer came out. No one seemed to see anything."

Ron eyed Bane. "Sounds like you have a suspect in mind. How can I help?"

"A man I helped convict for robbery and manslaughter got out of prison last week. He has carried a grudge against me a long time. I believe he's on the island. I'd like you to see if you can get hold of his agriculture form to see where he's staying." Bane told him about Zimmer.

"Whoa, buddy, you don't need to confront an ex-con. That is a job for me and mine."

He would have to confide in Ron. They had gone to school together and had been friends since first grade. Bane could only pray Ron kept it to himself. "There's more, but you can't tell headquarters."

Ron put his cup down. "I don't think I can promise that. Do you know about another crime?"

Bane exhaled and sat back in his chair. "If you tell anyone, someone I love could lose her life. I need you to promise me, brah."

Ron's green eyes widened. "Is this about Eva?"

He should have known Ron would guess. The man was no slouch when it came to investigations. "Yeah. She's been kidnapped. Leia has received a total of two calls from the kidnapper. He told her she had to break our engagement or he'd kill Eva."

"I see why you think it's Zimmer then. This is someone with a personal vendetta." Ron's expression hardened. "I bet Eva's terrified."

"I don't know. She's very trusting, and if the guy is nice to her, she'll take it with a smile. Leia's a mess, though. And Eva will start missing her family very soon. I have to find her."

Ron tapped his fingers on the table. "And if he listed his address on the form . . ."

"Exactly. We can find him and rescue Eva."

"I'll get a warrant for that form. Buddy, you really should have reported this. The entire force was out last night looking for her. The officers won't be happy they were misled."

"They weren't! I didn't know myself until early this morning."

"Leia didn't even tell you? Whoa."

Bane picked up his cup. "Yeah, can't say I was happy about it. Kind of a slap in the face." He hadn't wanted to admit his feelings to his siblings because he wanted them to love Leia. It felt safer somehow to talk to his longtime friend. "I gotta be honest — it's starting to make me wonder how much she really loves and trusts me."

Ron's gaze was sober when he nodded. "I can understand that. You talk to her about this?"

"Not much. She was already upset about Eva, and I didn't want to add to it."

"Brah, it'll have to get out in the open. The last thing you want is to go into a marriage that isn't right."

"I know. Once we find Eva, we'll talk it out and I'll decide what to do."

"So the wedding is off for now?"

Bane nodded. "That was the kidnapper's main demand, and he is checking up on her. He called her at midnight and told her he knew we hadn't canceled the food order."

"How'd he know where you'd ordered the catering?"

Bane shrugged. "No idea. Maybe he called around. There aren't that many catering places on the island."

"Or maybe it's not Zimmer at all. It could be someone local."

Bane hadn't even considered it could be someone else. "Like who?"

"Hard to say." Ron swallowed the last of his coffee. "I'll do some digging."

"And keep it to yourself?"

He stood and turned his cap around the right way. "For now. But if we haven't found her in the next few hours, I'll have to ask for help. You know the first few hours of a kidnapping are critical. I don't feel good about not reporting it even now."

"I know." Bane rose and tossed his cup into the trash. "Give me until morning."

Six

The back of Leia's neck prickled, and she whirled on the sidewalk along the back side of the Grand Hyatt by the ocean. The hotel had brought out all kinds of Christmas decorations, from giant wreaths to towering snowmen. A few tourists looked at her from their lounges around the saltwater lagoon, then went back to their books. She examined each one with care, but no one looked suspicious. She could have sworn someone was staring at her.

Where was her sister? She was frantic to find Eva after that phone call. Eva was so scared, and Leia felt helpless to rescue her. Maybe she should call the police. Even though the call had come up Unknown, the police might be able to trace it. But the man's threats left her frightened at the possible consequences.

She was hot and itchy from the sun, and the lagoon water looked refreshing. Averting her gaze, she resumed her stride toward Poipu Sands. The popular condos would be filled with tourists. She turned to walk to the lobby and heard her name. Turning, she saw Bane running toward her.

Her pulse leaped and she rushed to meet him. "You found her?"

He shook his head. "Sorry, honey. But I just got a call from Ron. He's got an address."

"Already?" She grabbed his hand, then realized they might be seen and quickly dropped it and stepped back. "Where?"

"A house in Poipu Kai, back along the green belt. Let's go."

It warmed her that he'd come to find her first without going straight there. Eva would need her if she became frightened. She hurried with him along the path to the houses fronting the green belt. Maybe Eva would be in her arms in just a few minutes.

They paused when they reached

where the sidewalk split. "Do we have backup? What if he has a gun?"

Bane patted his pocket. "I'm prepared."

She looked around the green belt. Some people jogged along the walk, others strolled with their dogs on leashes. The lush vegetation shimmered with color and fragrance, and Christmas lights adorned the shrubbery. The feeling of being watched persisted, but she saw no one staring in their direction. The sea breeze blew her hair into her face, and she plaited it while she waited for Bane.

She followed him when he set off on the right fork of the walk, toward Keleka Road where beautiful homes lined the shaded streets. "He paid some bucks to rent back in here."

"Yeah. Wonder where he got the money after being in prison." Bane paused and surveyed the house, a single-story plantation style with a wide front porch and beautiful vegetation in the yard. "There's a car in the drive."

"I noticed." She wanted to march to the door and demand her sister, but the wide windows would reveal who stood on the porch. The guy was liable to appear with a gun. She tugged on Bane's hand and pulled him behind a large palm tree. "I don't want him to see us. I think you should call Mano so you have backup."

Bane glanced at his cell when the text alert dinged. "Ron just drove through Koloa so he'll be here in ten minutes. He's going to meet us here. We can stake it out while we wait."

Pacing seemed like a bad idea in case they were seen, so to corral herself, she settled on the stiff, springy turf and clasped her knees to her chest. "What did you tell Ron? He just thinks it's about vandalism, right?"

He shook his head. "I told him the truth. All of it."

Her stomach plunged. "I assumed you told him about the tire slashing. The kidnapper said no police."

His dark eyes were expressionless. "I had to tell Ron. He knew there was more going on than what I was revealing. I needed his help tracking down Zimmer. He wouldn't give me the address otherwise."

She got to her feet and brushed flecks of grass from her hands. "I trusted you not to tell them. See, this is why I kept it from you in the first place. You law enforcement types stick together. If Eva dies, it's your fault!"

Shaking, she started to walk away, but he grabbed her forearm. "That's a lousy thing to say, Leia. I'm trying to save your sister. I love her too, you know. Statistics show bringing in the police is the best way to retrieve a kidnapped victim. You think you're capable of getting her back by yourself? I thought that's why you finally told me. You knew you couldn't do it alone. Well, I can't do it alone either."

He was right. His touch on her arm made her skin tingle. She pressed herself against him and buried her face in his shirt. His heart pounded hard under her ear. She tipped her face up to his. "I'm sorry, but I'm so scared."

His hand smoothed her hair. "Shh, shh. It's going to be all right, Leia." His lips brushed hers.

Her hands bunched into his shirt, and she kissed him back, drawing in the strength she needed. Bane was here. His sheer force of will would make sure Eva survived this.

He lifted his head and cupped her face in his hands. "As soon as Ron gets here, we'll go in. She'll be back with us very soon."

She nodded. "We have to move fast. She called me just before you came to get me and said he'd hurt her."

His hand fell away. "Wait a minute. Eva called you? Why didn't you tell me? How badly is she hurt?"

"We had a lead, so that was more important." She bit her lip. "I think he just squeezed her arm. She sounded panicked but okay."

"What'd she say? Did she give you any clues on her whereabouts?"

She shook her head. "She said there were no other houses around, so it was somewhere out of town. There are close neighbors here. She sounded so scared and kept begging me to come get her." Her voice broke. "She's depending on me to save her, and I'm so afraid he'll kill her if we don't do what he says."

Her cell phone rang, and her heart plunged when she pulled it out and looked at the screen. *Unknown.* "It's him." She swallowed hard, then answered the call. "Hello."

A scream reverberated through the phone, then her sister cried out, "Leia, help me!"

"Eva!" Her sister's voice was loud enough for Bane to hear too. "Let her go!"

He winced and looked toward the house. *I'm going in,* he mouthed.

She shook her head and held up one finger. He'd need backup. "Are you there?"

"Just remember, everything that happens from here on out is your fault," the electronic voice said. "You're with Bane now, aren't you? You told him, didn't you? All the wedding cancellations were just a trick to throw me off, but I'm too smart for you."

The phone went dead. Leia stared up at Bane. "He's hurting her! I bet he caught her with his cell phone."

Bane looked over her shoulder. "There's Ron. We're going in. Stay here."

"I'm coming with you!"

Ron's car door opened and he got out. "This the house?" His gaze flicked to Leia, then back to Bane.

Bane nodded. "And Leia just got a call from Eva. She was screaming." His jaw flexed and his eyes narrowed. "He'll pay for that."

Leia could still hear her sister's screams. "Let me go to the door first. You two can circle around the back. I don't think he'll feel threatened if I go up alone."

Bane began to shake his head but Ron nodded. "Makes sense. We'll wait until you're inside. Keep him away from the back of the house if you can."

"I don't want her hurt," Bane said.

"I'm not going to stand here and argue. I want my sister back." *Please, God, let her be okay.*

Leia headed up the driveway with more confidence than she felt. Keeping her gaze fastened on the door, she marched up the steps and rang the bell.

At first there was no answer. She rang again, then rapped hard on the door.

"Coming," a gruff voice called out.

The door swung open, and she saw a burly man about six feet tall. He had thick black hair that was unruly as though he'd just gotten out of bed, though it was afternoon. He wore a T-shirt and loose-fitting denim shorts. His feet were bare. She thought he was probably in his early forties.

"I've come for my sister."

His hazel eyes clouded. "Your sister? Who the heck are you? There's no woman here."

"You're Dennis Zimmer, right?"

He nodded. "So what?"

"You kidnapped my sister. I know she's in there, and I want her back right now."

He held up his hands. "Kidnapping? Whoa, listen, I've turned over a new leaf. In fact, I'm only here to apologize to a guy. I don't know anything about a kidnapping."

She believed him. Her heart sank. "Then you won't mind if I look around the house and make sure?"

He stepped out of the way. "Suit yourself. You won't find anyone here but me."

Bees buzzed around the pikake and gardenias lining the wide plantation porch, and the scent of flowers filled the air. Bane stood on the wide porch with his hands in the pockets of his shorts. He couldn't deny he was tense just being in Zimmer's presence, even though Leia assured him he didn't have anything to do with Eva's disappearance.

Zimmer stood by the door, next to the Aloha sign hanging on the siding. He looked older and more sober than the last time. Prison had changed him. Gone was the devil-may-care light in his eyes and the contemptuous sneer he usually wore.

Leia touched Bane's arm. "He

has something to say to you."

Zimmer took a deep breath. "Yeah, I just want to tell you I'm glad I went to prison. So I came here to thank you for making sure I paid for my crimes."

Bane blinked. "I don't get it. You swore to get even with me for sending you there."

Zimmer shuffled a little in his bare feet. "I know, and I'm sorry. I was a different man then. I've changed. Started going to a Bible study at the prison and, well, I see things differently now. I caused harm to a lot of people, and I can't make amends for most of what I did, especially for Dalton's death."

Ron was beside Bane, and he glanced at his friend but said nothing.

Bane nodded. "Have you seen his family?"

Zimmer winced, his hazel eyes filling with pain. "Yeah, his wife didn't want to hear anything I had to say. I don't blame her. Not much I can do to bring her husband back."

The guy seemed genuine. "I'm glad to hear you've changed. How long are you here for?"

"A week. Figured if I was going to spend the money to come, I'd see the island."

Where had he gotten that kind of money? "You here alone?"

"Yeah, though I'm seeing someone. She's coming tomorrow and staying in a condo on Shipwreck

Beach. She paid for my trip." He looked down at the floor. "She, uh, she's my lawyer, and she had a lot to do with turning my life around."

The last of Bane's suspicions melted away. "I hope you have a great trip. We'd better be going, though. We still need to find Eva." He took Leia's hand, and they started down the steps with Ron on their heels.

They reached Ron's car. "I was sure he'd slashed my tires. You think it was a random act, Ron?"

Ron shook his head. "Anything's on the table now."

"It happened the afternoon Eva was kidnapped, so it seemed likely they might be related."

"And it's the reason you assumed

whoever has done this is after you, right?"

Bane nodded. "So it's possible I was on the wrong trail all along. Actually, I was since I thought it was Zimmer who slashed my tires."

Ron glanced at Leia, who'd been unnaturally quiet. "You have any enemies, Leia? Where are you from?"

Leia's fingers curled more tightly around Bane's. "I live on Moloka'i. I don't have any enemies I know of."

Ron shrugged. "Okay, it was just a thought. I'll poke around and see if I can find out anything."

Bane looked back at the house. "You know it's not entirely true you have no enemies, Leia. We share a couple of common enemies from that fiasco about the artifacts. The henchmen might be out of jail now. Their sentences were lighter."

She went white, then nodded. "Moe Fletcher and Gene Chambers. Can we find out if they're out of jail?"

Ron nodded. "Let me make a call."

Bane glanced back toward the house. "They were in the same prison as Zimmer. Let's see if he met either of them. Wait here. He might know something about them."

Birds chirped from the avocado trees as he hurried back to the house. Zimmer was sitting at the lanai table and rose when he saw him.

Bane stopped on the bottom step. "I had one more question. I thought of someone who hates both of us, and I wouldn't be surprised if they were already out of prison. Did you meet Moe Fletcher or Gene Chambers?"

Zimmer's eyes widened. "Fletcher was my cell mate. Bad character, very bad. We got into a few scuffles, and I thought he'd kill me in my sleep some night."

"Is he still there?"

Zimmer shook his head. "He was released the month before me." His mouth hardened. "He talked about making a couple pay for putting him behind bars. That wouldn't be the two of you, would it?"

"Probably. I'll see if I can find out if he's on the island. *Mahalo* for your help." Bane bounded down the steps to the walk.

"I'll call if I hear anything. I know the kinds of places he's apt to hang out," Zimmer called after him.

Fletcher would pay for hurting Eva.

SEVEN

Bane was quiet as they drove toward Lihue to meet with Ron. Leia gazed out the window at the mountains rising on either side of the road as they left the tree tunnel. A light rain splattered the windshield, and she pressed her forehead against the glass. Dark clouds rolled in atop the mountaintops, and the wind picked up, stirring the palm fronds and the monkeypod tree leaves. The weathermen had predicted a cold front with accompanying rain. She could only pray Eva was safely inside somewhere. Her sister's screams reverberated in her head. Was she being tortured? Was she dead?

Leia couldn't tell what Bane was thinking. He'd been different since he found out she'd kept the kidnapper's call from him. Still concerned and solicitous but in a remote way, as if she was just another woman he was trying to help.

She turned back around to look at him. He stared straight ahead at the road. "Talk to me, Bane."

He glanced from the road, then back. "What do you want to talk about?"

The lump in her throat felt like a conch shell. "Us. There is still an us, isn't there?"

He drummed his fingers on the steering wheel, then shrugged. "You sure you want to get into this now, Leia?" His voice was tight as though he had hold of his emotions in a death grip.

"We have a twenty-minute drive before we get to the police station, so yes. We have time to discuss the way you've hardly looked at me or touched me, let alone kissed me. If I touch you, you kiss me back, but you haven't initiated anything." She laid her hand on his arm and could feel the response through his skin. He might not want her touch to mean anything, but it still did.

She wished the car were stopped so she could grab him by the shoulders and *make* him look her in the eye. She wanted to see into his heart, into the depths of his soul the way she used to.

He pressed his lips together, then exhaled. "It's been hard getting past being abandoned again."

Her cheeks burned as if he'd slapped her. "I never abandoned you."

"It felt like it. It was my mother all over again. One minute she was there and the next she'd run off with some guy. The way I saw things changed. I thought she loved me, then she walked away."

She removed her hand from his arm and clasped her hands together in her lap to keep them from trembling. "What does that have to do with Eva's kidnapping?"

They passed several houses decorated for Christmas, the lights shining out in the storm. Christmas. This felt like anything but Christmas. He still hadn't answered her. "Bane?"

His jaw clenched. "You shut me out the same way. I realized I didn't know you as well as I thought I did. Just like my mother, you were hiding things from me. If you want the truth of it, I'm hurt, Leia. Hurt you wouldn't tell me your deepest fears and feelings, and I'm afraid of what that means. I thought we had a bond that was special. Now I find it wasn't anything nearly as unique as I thought. We have passion, not denying that. Anytime you touch me, I want you close. But passion is nothing without trust."

Her eyes burned, and the boulder in her throat grew. She'd never thought how this might hurt him. "I'm sorry, Bane. I panicked. Can't you understand how that could happen?"

"Your first inclination should have been to turn to me, but it wasn't. And that kills me inside, just kills me." His voice was low and hoarse.

He shot a glance her way, and she nearly groaned from the pain in his eyes. What had she done? "I love you, Bane. You know I do. I'm only whole when we're together. It was my first inclination to talk to you, but I was so scared of what he might do. I wanted to tell you."

He grimaced. "It doesn't look that way, babe."

At least he was still calling her babe. "Do you love me?"

He gripped the wheel so tightly his knuckles went white. "You know I do. But what kind of marriage will we have if I'm always worried you're going to run out on me like my mom?"

She reached over and touched his forearm. It was rock hard from his grip on the steering wheel. "I would never leave you! You have to know that."

He shot her another look. "Do I? You sent me away once before. And you haven't exactly been pushing to get to the 'I dos.' This has been the longest engagement on record."

"It's only been a year." When she moved her hand to his face, he flinched a little. She brushed his thick black hair out of his eyes. "You're my world, Bane. I can't lose you. Please, you have to understand. I panicked, pure and simple. It made sense to follow what he said to get Eva back."

"Did it?" At least he didn't move his head away. "I'll have to take some time and think about this. There hasn't been an opportunity with our search for Eva. Right now, I guess you could say the wedding is truly off unless I can wrap my head around all of this."

She let her hand fall away as she absorbed the shock. On one level she understood his hurt, but why couldn't he see this was her *sister,* a sister who was really a child in spite of her actual age? "You don't think my first responsibility should have been to Eva?"

He skewered her with a glance. "We are supposed to be one. You split us into two when you shut me out. That's rejection, Leia. I'm trying to assimilate it, but it's hard to swallow."

An unspoken *if ever* hovered between them. The hurt went deep in him, deeper than she'd realized. All his childhood abandonment pain had resurged, and it was her fault.

Christmas revelers lined Rice Street waiting for the parade and the kickoff of the annual Festival of

Lights. The sun hung low in the sky, and Bane drove on through town out to Kalapaki Bay where they were to meet with Ron. He parked down the street.

Leia hadn't said much after they'd talked. He still felt raw and unsettled. There had been tears in her eyes, and he had to admit his heart had leaped when she said she loved him. And he knew she did, in her own way maybe. But he no longer was sure her kind of love was the lasting kind that would see them through ups and downs. At least it didn't appear to be.

He pulled the key from the ignition and glanced at her from the corner of his eye. Her long brown hair was in a braid that hung over one shoulder. He'd hoped to see it spill over a white nightgown on their wedding night. That might not happen now.

He opened his door. "Ron said he'd meet us at his house just down the street. We'll walk instead of park in his drive, just in case it tips off the kidnapper."

"There he is." Leia pointed out Ron standing along the side of the road.

When Ron saw he had their attention, he started off at a brisk pace down the street. They waited a couple of minutes, then followed. When he entered a small single-story house, they went up the walk and rang the bell.

He opened it immediately and

ushered them into a small living room. The sofa and chairs were leather, and seashells and other beach decor lightened the dark furniture. A small Christmas tree was on a table by the window. The seashell decorations were all white.

"Have a seat." He motioned to the sofa. "I have a lead on your guys. They both arrived here last week from Honolulu. They did not fill out the line of the form with their location here, but Fletcher has a cousin who lives here." Ron held up his hand when Bane started to speak. "The cousin lives in Waimea. Even if Fletcher's not there, we might get a lead on his where-abouts."

Bane frowned. "But wouldn't his

probation officer have to know where he is?"

"You'd think so, but I called his probation officer. He had no idea Fletcher or Chambers left O'ahu."

"So they're both in violation of probation," Leia said.

"Yep. Which is good for us. I ordered a warrant for their arrest for violation of parole." Ron's voice was grim. "I've got an officer on his way to the house now."

Leia leaped to her feet. "What? I want to be there to protect Eva. You should have called us and told us to head that way instead of here."

"Calm down," Ron said. "All the guy is going to do is ask if the cousin's heard from Fletcher. It will be all about probation. The other reason I didn't send you that way is I read the report of a brawl in a bar here in town last night. The perp who started the fight escaped, but his description sounds a lot like Fletcher. And I have a picture from the surveillance footage at the bar." He pulled out his iPhone and showed a photo to them.

Bane took one look and nodded. "That's Fletcher all right. So he's here in Lihue?"

"Maybe. But I don't think he's in Waimea. Could be in Kapaa." Ron's cell phone rang, and he answered. "Parker." He listened, drumming his fingers on his knee, then he pulled a pen and pad from his pocket and jotted down something. "Got it, *mahalo.*" He grinned and punched his phone. "We got him. The cousin said Fletcher was staying with a friend here in Lihue. A condo complex about ten minutes away."

Leia looked toward the door. "Let's go!"

Ron nodded. "We'd better hurry. My boss thinks Fletcher knows he's been spotted. He might take her and run."

She grabbed Bane's hand and tugged him up, and he couldn't stop the surge of emotion filling his chest at her touch. If he could, he would rip these feelings out, but it would be harder than he imagined to root out the love. Maybe he never would.

He pulled his hand away and followed her out the door.

The sun was setting over the water when they exited the house. A car turned the corner and drove toward them. The blue Chrysler's headlamps came on, then the tires squealed as the driver tromped on the accelerator. The car sped toward them. At first Bane wasn't concerned, then the vehicle veered as though it was going to jump the curb and careen down the sidewalk.

He grabbed Leia's hand and shoved her toward the trees. "Run!"

He raced after her toward a large monkeypod tree festooned with lights. The engine whined behind him, and he heard a thump. Glancing behind, he saw the car leap the curb and head toward the field where they were. "He's trying to run us down!"

He grabbed Leia and propelled her faster to the huge tree trunk. They both clung to the backside of the tree. When he peered around the tree, he stared straight into the face of the man they sought — Moe Fletcher. A maniacal grin stretched across his face.

The car barely missed the tree, then zoomed away. But not before Bane caught a glimpse of white-blond hair and Eva's terrified eyes.

EIGHT

Leia was shaking as Bane helped her up. "I think I saw Eva! Is that possible?"

Bane nodded, his mouth a grim line. "I saw her clearly." His gun out, Ron ran toward them as the car careened around the corner. "Are you all right? Did you see the driver?"

Leia nodded, still shuddering at the look on his face. "It was Fletcher." She clasped her arms around herself.

"Let's go! We might be able to catch him." Ron motioned for them to jump in his car with him.

Bane got into the backseat with her. "You're trembling." He put his arm around her. But there was no real warmth in the embrace, at least none Leia could detect. It was like being hugged by a brother or a friend. He'd pulled out all the stops to put up a barrier between them, but she *knew* he still loved her. Even though they were close to getting Eva back, Leia wanted to bury her face in her hands and cry. What would her life be like without Bane in it? It would be like never being able to sit on the sand with the sun on her face. Could she do anything to change his mind?

She curled her fingers into her palms and looked out at the Christmas lights along Rice Street. Once Eva was safely home, she would do everything in her power to show him she loved him. If she had it to do over again, she would do it all differently. He'd been right about the police. They needed Ron to find Eva. He'd been right about everything.

In the dark, taillights disappeared around the corner ahead of them. She leaned forward. "Is that them?"

Ron accelerated. "I think so."

She gripped Bane's hand as the car zoomed ahead. Residents lined the streets, waiting for the Christmas parade to start, and several shouted and shook their fists at them. The speed limit was only twenty through here, and no one on the island drove more than forty-five anywhere, not even the highways.

They followed him out of town, then the lights turned into Smith's Luau. She pointed. "There's the car, but why would he go there?"

Bane leaned forward. "The garden is large, and there will be a lot of people. Maybe he thinks he can lose us."

"Not with Eva. She'll scream the minute she gets out of the car."

But the car ahead of them drove past the luau. Bane pointed. "He's going to the river."

Leia caught a glimpse of her sister's blond hair in the security light before she was hustled from sight and pushed into the bottom of a boat. "Hurry! He's getting away."

"I'm going as fast as I can," Ron said. "The accelerator is on the floorboard."

The tires skidded as they reached the parking lot, and Ron pulled the car to a stop under a light. The smell of burning rubber wafted up her nose as she threw open the door and clambered out on her side. "Eva!" A faint scream came to her ears. "We're coming, Eva!"

Leia's lungs constricted as she ran to the canoes. The other boat had disappeared in the darkness. Bane was beside her untying the canoe and grabbing an oar.

"I've called for backup," Ron

yelled. He grabbed her arm and helped her into the canoe, then followed her.

The canoe rocked and she grabbed at the side. "Hurry, Bane!"

He tossed the rope into the canoe and stepped onto the bottom of the boat. She leaned over so he could get to the back of the boat. "I'll steer, you paddle."

Bane's muscular arms flexed as he bent into the rowing. She moved the paddle and guided them to the center of the Wailua River. She'd never been on the river at night, and it was disorienting not to see the bank very well. The gnarled trees seemed to be reaching for them as if to stop them from catching up with Fletcher and Chambers.

Her muscles tightened at what sounded like a scream ahead. "What if he's drowning her?"

Bane redoubled his efforts at the oar. There was a splash ahead. Leia stood and strained her eyes trying to see. "Eva!"

The hair stood on end on her neck at the blood-curdling scream that slashed the silence. "Eva!"

Her sister couldn't be more than twenty feet ahead, but it was a dark, cloudy night and Leia could barely see her hand in front of her face.

"Leia, sit down! You're going to tip us." Bane's voice was hoarse.

She ignored his order and kicked off her slippers. "I'm going in! Ron, you take the stern."

"Leia, no! We're nearly there."

"He's killing her!" she screamed when her sister cried out again.

Without wasting another moment, she dove into the river. The warm water closed over her head, and she kicked to the surface, then struck out with strong strokes. Splashing sounded ahead to her right, and she veered that direction, shouting her sister's name. The other canoe loomed out of the darkness, just five feet away. She saw no figures in the boat, so they all must be in the water.

She treaded water and tried to get her bearings by sound alone. Frantic splashing came from the other side of the canoe. She submerged to swim without noise to the other side. Her head broke the surface, and she saw movement to her right. Then an oar came out of nowhere and struck her head.

The pain made her gasp, and her vision began to dim. Her muscles slackened, but before her eyes closed, Fletcher's grinning face mocked her.

"Hardheaded, stubborn woman," Bane muttered, throwing the oar to the bottom of the canoe.

"She's got guts." Ron's voice came out of the darkness, and a shadow moved as he shifted. "You picked a good one there."

Bane kicked off his slippers and slipped into the water. The least amount of noise he could make, the better. The water was a silken caress around his limbs as he did a noiseless breaststroke toward where Leia had disappeared.

"Let go of my sister!" Eva yelled.

Her voice was to his right, but Bane circled around the other way. He had a sixth sense of another presence in that direction. Fletcher or Chambers? He kicked his legs and propelled himself through the calm water. A rooster crowed from the bank to his left. The sound oriented him to the distance to the shore. About fifteen feet. Could they be taking Eva and Leia to the other bank?

He paused and tried to see. Something moved about five feet away.

After inhaling a deep breath, he dove deep and kicked toward the sound. His outstretched hand touched a thick ankle. His fingers closed around it, and he pulled down with all his might and dove hard for the bottom.

The man kicked to try to break Bane's grip, but Bane gritted his teeth and hung on. He was an expert free diver and had better lung capacity than this out-of-shape ex-con. He held the man to the bottom until he quit struggling and air began to bubble from the guy's mouth, then Bane shot to the top with the limp figure and swam to the shore. He staggered to the shore and threw the man to the mud.

When he started to turn to dive back to find Leia, the moon came from behind a cloud. The dim glow touched the face of a figure lying along the bank. "Leia!"

In two steps he was by her side. He knelt next to her and touched her face. It was still warm, and her chest rose and fell with her breaths. "Thank God you're alive."

"Such a touching reunion," a sneering male voice said behind him.

He whirled and saw the barrel of a gun aimed at his chest. Behind it was Fletcher's gloating face. "The police know about you, Fletcher. And so does your parole officer."

The man shrugged. "So what? I'll be dead in three months. Thanks to you two, I got hepatitis in prison. Destroyed my liver."

"It's not our fault you went to jail. You chose to break the law."

Fletcher bared his teeth. "You think you're so much better than everybody. But look who's in control now!" He gestured with the gun. "Roll Chambers over. I want to see if you killed him."

"He's not dead." Bane stepped over to where the inert man lay and prodded him with a bare foot, then rolled him over. Chambers moaned, but his eyes stayed closed. "See?"

"I'm through with him anyway." Fletcher turned the gun on his partner's head, and a muffled shot rang out. "You're next, but first we're going to have a little fun."

Bane's ears rang. "What did you do to Leia? And where's Eva?"

"You'll see soon enough. Grab your girlfriend and come with me."

Backup was coming. Ron would be along with more police any minute. But would he look this way, or would they search the water first? Bane had to keep them all alive until he could get the gun or get help. He moved to Leia's side and sat her up.

Her head rolled to the side but her eyes fluttered open. There was no recognition in her eyes at first, then her lids flew open. "Bane! Where's Eva?" Her voice was groggy.

"We're about to find out. Can you

stand?"

"I-I think so."

He helped her to her feet and supported her as they moved along the path between two giant trees. "Where are we going?"

"Shut up and walk." Fletcher prodded Bane's back with the gun.

Bane glanced around for something to use as a weapon. He'd never be able to grab a branch before Fletcher put a bullet in him. A man with nothing to lose was the most dangerous of all. No wonder Fletcher hadn't cared about breaking his parole.

They reached a clearing in the trees, and a small building crouched at the back. Back in the nineties, Hurricane 'Iniki had blown off most of the roof and the windows and the door, but it still stood. A light shone out of the broken glass of the windows. He saw a blond woman tied up and quickened his pace, urging Leia faster. She would want to make sure Eva was all right.

They stumbled through the shack's doorway. Chicken feathers and debris littered the interior. Eva sat bound to a chair at a table that leaned drunkenly to one side, two legs off.

Eva lifted her head at the noise, and her eyes widened. "Leia!"

Leia leaped forward and reached her sister. She knelt beside her. "You're alive." Her fingers tore at the ropes, but she made little headway on the tight knots.

Bane turned to face his captor. He had to find a way to disarm him. He sidled toward a table leg lying on the floor. "Why bring us here? Why not drown us?"

"I have something more fun in mind. Like letting Leia here watch her sister die. Then you can watch me shoot Leia. I'll save you for last, then wait for the police. I'm sure they're on their way."

Moe aimed the gun at Eva as Bane lunged for the table leg.

NINE

Leia stepped in front of her sister with her arms outstretched. She stared in horror as Fletcher took a step toward them. His finger moved on the trigger.

Bane seemed to sag forward as if he'd been hurt, then grabbed the chair leg by his feet. In one motion, he snatched up the chair leg and brought it around in an arc aimed at Fletcher's wrist. The wooden leg struck Fletcher's hand, but he managed to hang on to the gun.

Bane leaped onto him, and the two struggled over the weapon.

Leia turned back to her sister and tore into the ropes with new fury. The thick fiber cut into her fingertips but finally began to loosen. She unraveled one knot. There was grunting and cursing on the floor behind her as Fletcher fought to retain possession of the gun. Bane was bigger and stronger, though, so she could only pray he would prevail. The last knot gave way, and she yanked the bonds away from Eva's wrist, then lifted her sister to her feet.

She cupped Eva's face in her hands. "Let's get outside. Hurry."

Eva nodded and threw her arms around Leia. "You came."

"I told you I would." Leia quickly disentangled from Eva's embrace and supported her as they turned for the door. They had to get help.

Locked in struggle, Bane and Fletcher rolled toward her, and she pressed Eva forward even faster. Then they were through the doorway. The night air touched her face, but there was no sign of any police yet. She shoved Eva into the yard. "Scream as loud as you can! We have to get the police here."

She rushed back to help Bane. The only weapon she could see was the chair, so she picked it up and held it over her head, waiting for the right moment to use it. Outside, Eva was shrieking at the top of her lungs. Her scream was loud enough to call anyone within ten miles.

Bane landed a punch on Fletcher's face, then rolled on top of him and pinned his arms down. "Give it up, Fletcher," he panted. He'd lost the gun somewhere.

"Never!" Fletcher managed to get one hand loose, and he jabbed Bane in the chin.

Bane fell off, and Fletcher scrambled to his feet. He grabbed another broken piece of chair leg from the floor and waved it menacingly in Bane's direction. Neither man had possession of the gun, and Leia looked around for it. It had to be here somewhere. She finally spied it under the table, so she dove onto her stomach for it just as Fletcher made a swipe at Bane with the poker.

Bane feinted left, then his big hand grabbed the poker and yanked it out of Fletcher's grip. He tossed it aside and leaped at the other man again. Leia's fingers closed around the gun, and she backed out from under the table. The grit and debris on the floor bit into her knees.

She sat up breathlessly, then got to her feet with the gun pointed toward the struggling men. She didn't know how to use it, but it looked menacing. If only she could get it to Bane, but the two men were locked in mortal combat. Fletcher wouldn't give up unless he was unconscious or dead.

She hovered five feet away from

the struggling men. The discarded chair leg was at her feet, so she picked that up too and stood waiting for her chance to help.

Bane grunted as Fletcher rolled on top of him. Fletcher lifted Bane's head and slammed it against the floor. Bane's gaze locked with Leia's. *Shoot,* he mouthed.

Leia looked at the gun in her hand. What if she hit Bane? She wasn't that good of a shot. Fletcher smacked Bane's head down against the floor again. Bane flung out a hand as if stunned, but Leia caught his eye again. In an instant, she dropped the gun into his hand.

He brought it up and aimed it at Fletcher. "Back against the wall."

The glee faded from Fletcher's

face. He held his hands up and got to his feet.

Bane stood with his chest heaving. "Hand me that rope, would you?"

Leia dropped the poker and grabbed the rope. When she handed it to him, he grinned. "Annie Oakley, you're not."

"I have never held a gun before. I don't like it much."

"Glad we didn't have to use it." He tied up Fletcher and stepped back. "Eva okay?" Bane tipped his head to one side. "I can hear her screeching. Nothing wrong with those lungs at least. The police should be here any minute. They had to have heard her from the lake."

She heard some shouts. "I think that's them now." The fight seemed to have gone on forever, but she knew it couldn't have been longer than five minutes at the most. "Thank you for saving her, Bane. You were right. I needed you. I needed the police." She hesitated a moment. "I need to get to Eva."

She hurried away before he could answer.

An ambulance with flashing lights was outside the shack. Bane tried to stay out of the way under the spreading branches of an *'ohi'a* tree as police tromped back and forth gathering evidence, though they had plenty of witnesses that Fletcher shot Chambers. Kaia had picked up Leia and Eva and taken them back to the house so she could fuss over them. Mano stayed behind to ride home with Bane.

Bane couldn't forget the expression on Leia's face before she left. He wished they could go back to the way things were last week.

Mano's expression was grim when he joined Bane under the tree. "Pretty cold to shoot him in the head when he was unconscious."

"Chambers was going to kill us too. Fletcher says he's dying. The police say that's true. He had a run-in with another guy at the prison. The guy arranged for him to get stuck with a dirty needle, and he got a virulent form of hepatitis that ravaged his liver. He probably won't be alive in three months."

Bane watched as two police officers marched Fletcher off with his hands cuffed behind his back. They put him in a police car. He stared balefully back at Bane as the car pulled away down the dirt track.

"Scary guy," Mano commented. "You look a little beat up."

Bane touched his swelling eye. "Could have been worse."

"Yeah." Mano's perusal grew intense. "I don't like to pry, but are things okay between you and Leia? You both seemed a little tense."

"The wedding is off," Bane blurted out.

Mano went quiet. He scuffed his flip-flop in the dirt a moment, then shook his head. "Doesn't seem right, brah. I've never seen you happier than you've been with her. You want to talk about it?"

"What's to talk about? She shut me out of her life deliberately."

"Women process things differently than we do."

"Spoken by a man with a whole two years of marriage under his belt." Bane grinned to deflect any sting in his words, then his smile faded and he shook his head. "She lied to me, Mano. Let me believe — let all of us believe — Eva had likely drowned from jumping off the Point. She was willing to call off the wedding rather than trust me with the truth. That's hard to get past."

"This is about Mom, isn't it?"

Bane shrugged and grabbed his brother's forearm. "Let's get out of the way. We'll go down by the river."

Tree frogs set up a cacophony as they walked down to the river. The moon glimmered on the water, and fish splashed off to their left.

Bane and Mano settled on rocks along the water's edge. At least he wouldn't be overheard here. He didn't feel good talking about Leia where someone might hear. It was too personal.

He picked up a flat stone and sent it skipping across the water. "Do you trust Annie to never leave you?"

Mano inhaled sharply. "Well, sure. I wouldn't have married her if I didn't believe that."

"I'm not so sure about Leia. I thought I knew her. That I would be the first person she turned to in trouble, just like she is the first one I would turn to. Then I found out she lied. Again."

"What do you mean again?"

"I dated her once before. She didn't want to get too close because she intended to never marry and have kids. The genetic defects in her family. So Leia chose the easy way out and never talked to me about it. What kind of marriage would we have if she's afraid to talk to me about what matters?"

Bane's chest felt heavy. Life had been so full of hope and joy just last week. How could it have disintegrated into this morass of unhappiness so quickly?

"I kind of understand what happened, though, can't you? The guy convinced her Eva would die if she didn't do as she was told. She came from a traditional Hawaiian family. She's used to obeying authority. What would you have done if someone took Kaia and told you if you didn't follow his instructions, he'd kill her?"

Bane started to answer glibly, then paused to really consider the question. What would he do if his beloved sister were in the hands of some kind of maniac? Especially if she were handicapped and frightened like Eva? He'd want to get her back as quickly as possible. If the

159

kidnapper had said no police, would he have called the police immediately?

He shook his head. "I guess I wouldn't have told the police. But I would have told Leia."

"Even if you were told not to?"

"Even then. Together we would hatch a plan to make it appear we were following the guy's instructions, but we would have searched high and low for her."

"But you're, well, you. A big, capable guy with resources to track your sister down by yourself. Leia thought her best chance of getting her sister back was doing exactly what the kidnapper said. We know now he always planned to kill you both and intended to cause as much pain along the way as he could. If you let him break up you and Leia, he'll have won."

Bane picked up another rock and felt its smooth, round edges for a moment before he sent it skipping across the water. It skipped four times, then sank. Right now he felt like that stone — jittering over an unknown surface and headed for who knew where. But Leia was his compass and with her, he knew where he was headed.

He turned and looked at his brother. "I love her, you know."

"Of course you do. Otherwise this wouldn't have hurt so much. You can get past this, Bane. There are little hurts in any relationship, but you talk about it and work through them." Mano stood and extended his hand.

Bane took his brother's hand and got to his feet. "You're a good brother, brah."

"I know." Mano pointed at Bane's swelling eye. "Good thing I have the brains *and* the brawn in this family."

TEN

The guest room window was open, and the sweet scent of plumeria wafted in soothingly. Christmas lights festooned the palm tree outside the window and cast a comforting glow into the bedroom.

Leia tucked the clean white sheet around her sister, then smoothed the white-blond hair away from Eva's face. She leaned over to kiss her forehead. "Rest now, sweetheart. You're safe."

Eva's guileless blue eyes held

worry as she stared up into Leia's face. "Are you sad, Leia? You look sad."

Leia forced a smile. "I'm very happy you're home safe and sound. It was a scary thing for you to have to go through. But we're all okay now."

Eva nodded. "And the wedding will be soon. We have lots and lots to do. I need to try on my dress again."

She'd tried it on at least twenty times. The cornflower blue bridesmaid dress had lace flounces, and Eva loved to twirl in it like a princess.

Leia's smile faded. How did she tell Eva there would be no wedding? She wouldn't understand.

Tears prickled along the backs of Leia's eyes. "Um, about the wedding . . ."

A tap sounded on the door, and she turned to see Bane standing in the open doorway. Joy surged through her at the sight of his broad shoulders and thick shock of black hair. He needed a shave, but she'd never seen him look handsomer.

Now that she'd lost him.

Eva sat up and held out her arms. "Bane!"

He crossed the room in five strides and sat on the edge of the bed, then embraced her. "Hey, squirt. You don't look any the worse for wear."

"I am, though. Look." Eva

showed him her arm where lurid bruises shaped like fingers marred the pale skin.

His mouth flattened and his eyes narrowed. He shot a glance at Leia. "That'll heal up just fine."

Eva's fingers touched the bruise around his eye. "Fletcher hit you. He's a bad, bad man."

"The police will make sure he never hurts you again."

Leia studied him as he soothed her sister and kissed her good night. He seemed different somehow tonight. More relaxed without that harsh line to his mouth she'd seen for the past three days. She hovered near the bed until he gave Eva a final kiss, then rose and moved toward the door.

She followed him. "Good night, sweetheart."

"Night, Leia. Night, Bane." Her eyes closed, and Eva rolled to her side. "I didn't miss the wedding. Or Christmas."

Leia smiled and pulled the door shut as they exited the room. "I can't believe this is over." She glanced up at him. "Well, almost over. We still have some wedding plans to cancel. I need to call my parents and tell them not to fly over. And you —" She cut off what she was about to say when Bane put his fingers on her lips.

"I want to talk to you. Come with me." He led her through the living room and outside to the steps that went down to the ocean.

The sound of the sea rose in a crescendo with the storm surge still kicking up the waves. Whitecaps gleamed in the moonlight. It was a night very much like this one when Bane had proposed to her. He was still holding her hand. Did that mean anything, or was he merely being solicitous about her safety on the uneven ground?

They reached the *imu* pit area where his grandfather and his father's father before him had cooked the luau pig for generations. Someone had already lit a fire, though she saw no one around. Even his grandfather's house was dark and quiet. The old man had gone to bed long ago.

"Have a seat."

She settled on a log and looked out over the water. Hope was nearly impossible to kill in the spirit, though she tried to keep hold of the way hers wanted to rise in her chest.

He sat on the log next to her and reached behind him, pulling up his 'ukulele. His fingers strummed the strings for a few moments. She kept her gaze on the strong lines and planes of his face. He was so dear and so handsome. His strong legs stretched out past his shorts, and his feet were bare.

She swallowed hard. "Did you do all this? Light the fire and lay out the seating?"

He nodded, his dark eyes on her. "Mano talked some sense into me tonight. We're never going to see eye to eye about everything, babe. I'm going to do things that hurt you too, things you don't understand. But that doesn't mean I don't love you."

"I'm sorry I hurt you," she whispered. "I was operating on pure panic. I won't ever do that again, Bane, I promise."

"Even if you do, I'm going to love you through it." His gaze held hers. "I was wrong to push you away."

Tears welled in her eyes and blurred his face. He strummed the 'ukulele again and began to sing the song he'd written just for her, the one he'd sung the night he proposed. The Hawaiian song spoke of his great love and longing for her and ended with a proposal of marriage.

He laid the 'ukulele down on the sand. "Want to marry me after all?" His grin was teasing.

She leaped from the log and launched herself at him. They both fell onto the sand. His lips were salty with the sea when he kissed her. The heat between them was hotter than the sun at noonday, but she gave herself up to the passion in his kiss.

He pulled away first and gave a shaky laugh. "How much longer until that honeymoon?"

"Soon," she promised, and pulled his head back down for another kiss.

■ ■ ■ ■

Leia peeked out the window of the suite at the Hyatt. The big rollers flowing onto the beach were a perfect backdrop to the white tents festooned with red poinsettia wreaths. Twinkling lights added another Christmas touch. Leia had ducked inside the tents earlier and gawked at the tables decorated in red and gold for Christmas.

"I keep pinching myself." She turned to smile at Eva. "I can't believe this is really happening."

Her sister preened in her lacy blue dress. "Your hair is really pretty, Leia."

Leia glanced in the mirror. Eva had curled it all over, then Leia pulled it back from her face so it cascaded down her back. They'd pinned white pikake blossoms among the strands. "I love it too. I couldn't have done it without you."

"Can I get your dress now?" When Leia nodded, Eva moved to the closet and pulled out the gown.

Leia had made it herself. It was *kapa,* the traditional Hawaiian cloth made from mulberry bark. She'd worked on it for months, making sure the color was a soft white and the material was as supple as buckskin. She'd infused the fabric with pikake as well, and the sweet fragrance filled the room. The supple cloth was as white as she could make it with multiple bleachings in the sun, and she'd painted a blue plumeria along one hip. The color matched Eva's dress. The effect was unique and striking. At least she thought so. No one had seen it except for Eva.

Her sister helped her get the dress on without messing up her hair. She fastened the zipper in the back for Leia. When Leia spun around, Eva's eyes widened. "You are like the sun."

Leia's eyes filled with tears. "Thank you."

When the knock came on her door, she opened it and took her father's hand. "I'm ready."

His face beamed with pride as he looked her over. "I've never seen you more beautiful, honey. And this dress! I can't believe you made this by yourself. Your grandmother will be so proud. She's having a good day today too. I think she'll remember it."

The day couldn't have been more perfect. She took her father's right arm, and Eva took the left. "Let's get you married," he said.

People in the lobby of the hotel stopped and stared at her unique gown as she passed. Several took pictures, and she walked with her head erect, happy with her appearance for the first time in her life. Once they reached the beach, she took off her shoes and walked barefoot toward the arbor of poinsettias, greenery, and twinkling lights where her future waited. Friends and family lined both sides of the white runner that led to the minister. She smiled at her mother and sister.

One of Bane's friends played Wagner's "Bridal Chorus" on a 'ukulele. The crowd burst into applause and pointed out to sea. Leia turned to see an outrigger canoe closing rapidly on the wedding party. Two dolphins pulled it, and Mano was at the bow. He blew the traditional pu shell horn, then blew it again. The regal sound brought tears to her eyes.

Mano hopped overboard and swam to shore with the horn aloft, then, dripping wet, he stepped to his brother's side and winked at her.

Then she was there in front of

Bane. His eyes were wide as he looked her up and down. "Oh, babe," he whispered. "I'm speechless."

She smiled at the love in his eyes. She saw no one else in that moment. It was only Bane's warm brown eyes staring into her soul.

The minister cleared his throat. "In Hawai'i the lei is given as a sign of eternal aloha, a symbol of how you weave your lives together forever."

Bane took the elaborate pikake lei from Mano and placed it around her neck. Her fingers closed around the ti leaf lei in Kaia's hand, and she slipped it over Bane's head.

"As you weave your lives together, may you always trust one another and be united as you journey toward the eternity God has promised." The pastor glanced at her father. "Who gives this woman to be married to this man?"

Her father squeezed her hand, then looked at the minister. "Her mother and I do. And God himself." He transferred her hand to Bane's arm. "Take good care of her, son. She's most precious to me."

Bane's warm fingers closed over her hand. "And to me."

Together they stepped under the arbor. The ceremony passed in a blur as Leia looked into Bane's eyes and repeated the traditional vows. She wanted to remember these words and this moment forever, but she was mostly conscious of the press of his hand and the love in his eyes. The pastor spoke of the holiness of this night, and it seemed somehow even more fitting that their wedding was on Christmas Eve.

"Now I give you the traditional Hawaiian blessing," the minister said. "*E Ho'omau Maua Ke Aloha.* That means 'From this day, this night, forevermore together.' You may kiss the bride."

"Under the mistletoe?" Bane asked, sweeping her into his arms.

She hadn't realized there was mistletoe here, but she saw it as she tipped up her face to meet his. His lips came down on hers, softly at first, then with rising passion that spread heat through her chest, down her arms, and into her belly. The sensation was so intense she had to cling to him to keep from falling. When he lifted his head, she was breathless.

"I think I'd like you to do that again," she whispered.

His lips twitched. "I think you just gave me permission to kiss you like that all the time."

The 'ukulele sprang to life again as they turned to walk through the crowd of friends and family. Her face hurt from smiling so much as they accepted congratulations through the evening and mingled at the food tables. The party would run all night, but she suddenly wanted Bane all to herself. She led him off to a quiet corner.

"Is everything all right?"

Suddenly shy, she glanced down at her bare feet peeking out from under the hem of the dress. "Think you're strong enough to carry me to our room?"

"I think I can manage that." The glint in his eyes went from warm to lava hot. He swept her up and carried her toward the hotel amid the hoots and cheers of their guests.

Leia hid her face in his shoulder and gave one final wave to Eva. He carried her to the elevator amid the grins of the employees and guests of the hotel. They were the only ones in the elevator as it moved briskly to the sixth floor.

"Tired yet?" She brushed her lips

across his.

"Not even close." The ardor in his gaze intensified as the elevator doors opened.

Their suite was two doors down. She fumbled the key out of his pocket and unlocked it from her perch in his arms. He pushed into the suite and the door shut behind them.

This night would cement their love into a holy bond that would never be broken. Leia closed her eyes and clung to the promise of forever in his kiss.

READING GROUP GUIDE

1. Was Leia right to try to obey the kidnapper? Why or why not?
2. What is the difference between forgiving and forgetting after someone hurts you? Is it possible to forget?
3. Bane felt marriage had to be based on trust. Why is that important in a marriage?
4. Do we ever get over childhood hurts?
5. What do you think are the

biggest differences between
men and women?

ABOUT THE AUTHOR

RITA-finalist **Colleen Coble** is the author of several best-selling romantic suspense novels, including *Tidewater Inn* and the Mercy Falls, Lonestar, and Rock Harbor series.